D1451757

THE BOUNCY BABY BUNNY

by **Joan Bowden**

illustrated by **Patience Brewster**

A Golden Book • New York
Golden Books Publishing Company, Inc.,
New York, New York 10106

Text © 1974 Golden Books Publishing Company, Inc. Illustrations © 1999 by Patience Brewster. All rights reserved. Printed in Italy. No part of this book may be reproduced or copied in any form without written permission from the publisher. GOLDEN BOOKS®, A GOLDEN BOOK®, GOLDEN BOOKS FAMILY STORYTIME™, and G DESIGN™ are trademarks of Golden Books Publishing Company, Inc. Library of Congress Catalogue Card Number: 98-85511 ISBN: 0-307-10217-3   A MCMXCIX

This book has a reinforced trade binding.

Every morning, back in the woods, the bouncy baby
bunny played with his brothers and sisters. They leaped
in the air and raced through the trees and flowers.

Then they rolled down the hill, **roly-poly-over**. The bouncy baby bunny was always in front. He was the first to tumble into their hole for an afternoon nap.

One afternoon, the bouncy baby bunny could not get to sleep. He fidgeted and he fudgeted.

Then . . .

THUMP! WHUMP! BUMP!

He bounced his brothers and sisters out of bed.
The little rabbits didn't like that, not one bit.
"You are too bouncy for us," they complained.
"Go find someplace else to sleep!"

And that's just what the bouncy baby bunny did.
He found a beaver's home. It was not as comfortable
as a nice, dry rabbit burrow, and he could *not* get
to sleep. He fidgeted and he fudgeted. Then . . .

SPLISH! SPLOSH! SPLAT!

He bounced all the little beavers out of bed and into the pond.

Mother beaver didn't like that, not one bit. "You are much too bouncy for us," she cried. "Please find somewhere else to sleep!"

Off bounced the baby bunny.

Next he tried napping with a family of chipmunks.
But he was too wiggly to be welcome there.

Then he tried snuggling into a mouse's house.
But the mice made the twitchy bunny leave.

He even tried to get comfy in a woodchuck's hole.
But he ended up bouncing the animals out of bed.

The woodchucks didn't like that, not one bit. "You are much, *much* too bouncy for us!" they cried.

"SCOOT!"

"SCAT!"

"SHOO!"

And they chased him away.

The bouncy baby bunny felt very sad. He wished he were in his own snug home.

His brothers and sisters were wishing the same thing.
Because . . . back in their burrow, a mean old skunk had
forced his way in. "This is *my* hole now! Here I am, and
here I'll stay!" he said.

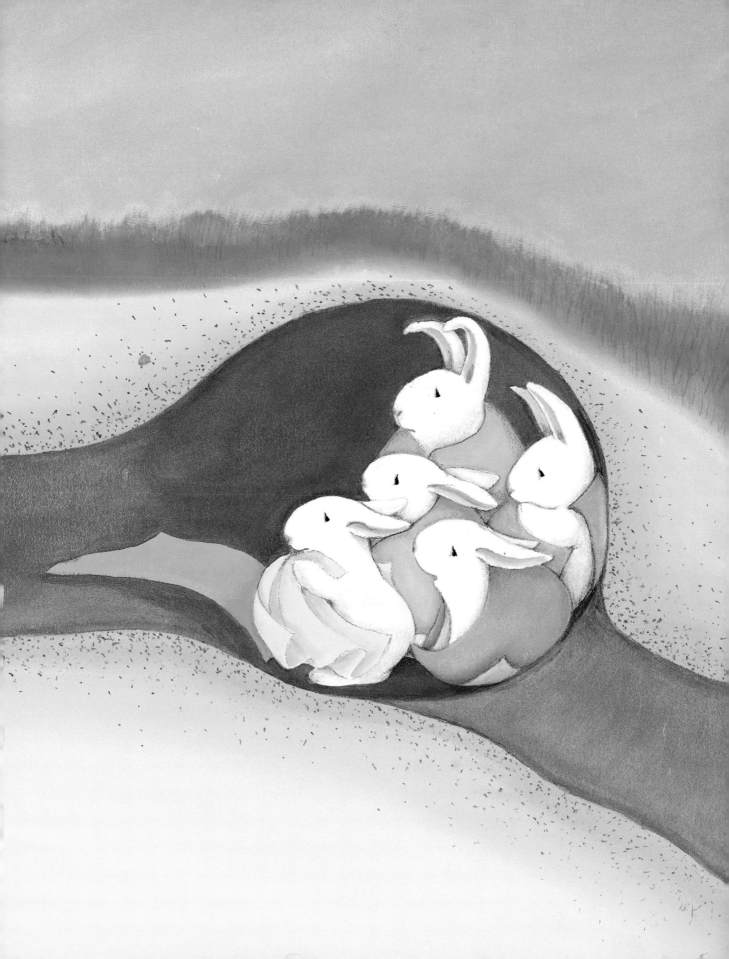

He rolled himself into a tight little ball and fell fast asleep.

The little rabbits tried to get rid of that old skunk. They were nice:

"Mr. Skunk, would you please go away?"

They were bossy: "Go away, skunk, NOW!"

They tried begging:

"PLEASE, PLEASE LEAVE SO WE CAN TAKE OUR NAPS!"

But that pesky skunk didn't listen.
He just rolled himself into a tighter ball
and began to snore.

The little rabbits didn't know what to do.
If only their bouncy little brother were there
to help them!

Where was he? Well, after being kicked out of so many homes, he had found an empty log to curl up in. Little did he know that the log belonged to a porcupine.

When the porcupine came home, he discovered the bouncy baby bunny fast asleep. "Who's that sleeping in my house?" he cried.

Then, before the bouncy baby bunny knew what was happening, the porcupine dove into the log and bounced the bunny out of bed!

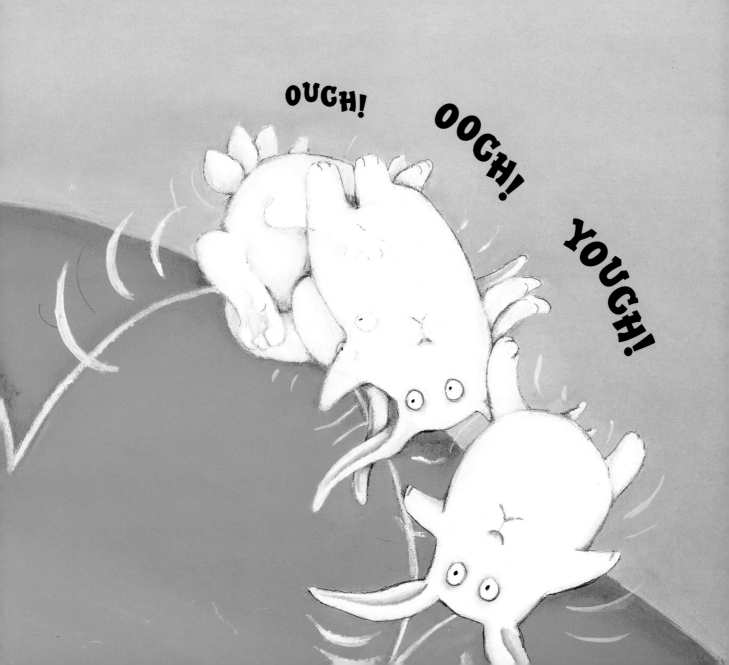

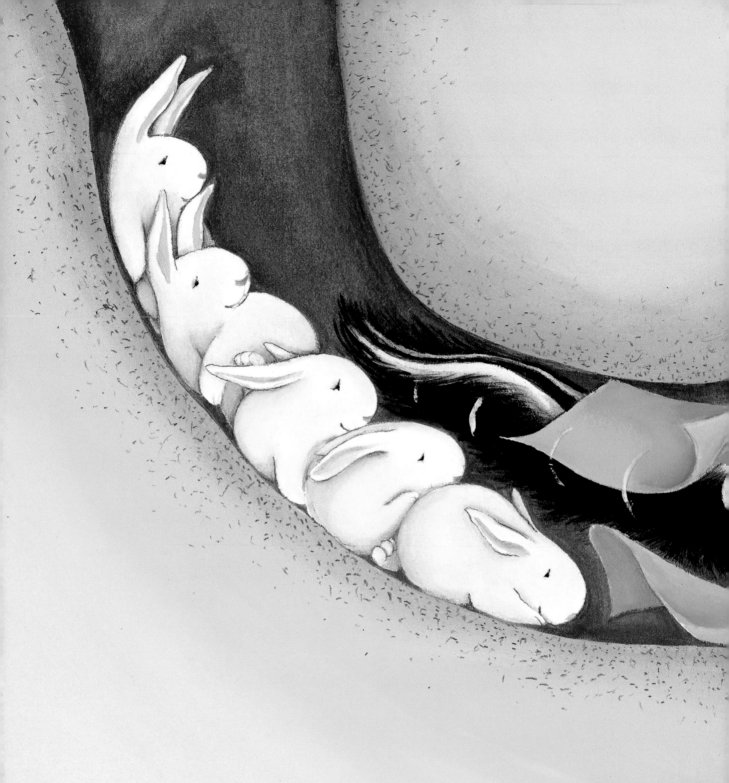

Out of the hollow log spun the bouncy baby bunny,
roly-poly-over, faster and faster, all the way down

the hill, until . . .

WHISH!   **WHOOSH!**   **WHOMP!**

He bounced right through his own front door . . .

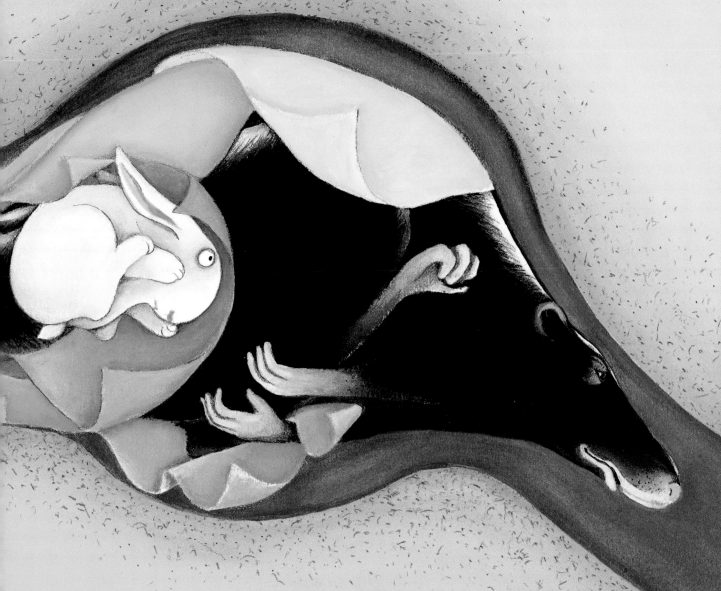

. . . and into the ornery old skunk. That skunk
shot through the back door like a bullet.

He rolled head over tail down the hill and landed smack-dab in the middle of a brambly patch.

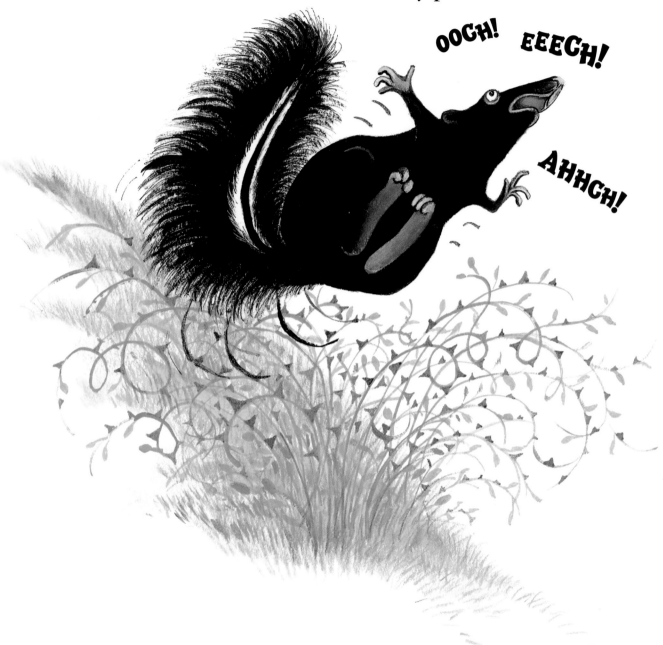

How those brambles hurt! The skunk scrambled out of the patch and ran far, far out of sight.

The baby bunny's brothers and sisters were very glad to see him. "You are not too bouncy for us," they said. "You are just right!"

The bouncy baby bunny was so happy he could have burst. *But . . .*

. . . he fell asleep instead!